I KILLED
FATHER CHRISTMAS

I KILLED FATHER CHRISTMAS

Anthony McGowan

WITH ILLUSTRATIONS BY
CHRIS RIDDELL

Barrington Stoke

First published in 2017 in Great Britain by
Barrington Stoke Ltd
18 Walker Street, Edinburgh, EH3 7LP

www.barringtonstoke.co.uk

Text © 2017 Anthony McGowan
Illustrations © 2017 Chris Riddell

A CIP catalogue record for this book is available
from the British Library upon request

ISBN: 978-1-78112-710-0

*To Gabe and Rosie –
my own Jo-Jo and Poo-face*

CONTENTS

Chapter 1

My List

It was Christmas Eve, and Mum and Dad were fighting again. Mum shouted at Dad and Dad shouted at Mum. I put the pillow over my head and tried to shut out the sound.

I felt bad because I was to blame. It was my fault. I'd been naughty.

Dad said I was greedy because my list for Father Christmas was so long. He said Father Christmas and the reindeer would be tired out if they had to carry all that. He said all my extra presents would mean Father Christmas might not be able to reach the poor children in far-off countries. And then he said Father Christmas didn't have very much money to spend on presents this year because the economy was so bad and nobody could be sure of their job any more.

"I don't care about poor children or the economy," I said. "I want a robot, and a racing car, and a helicopter that really flies."

But now I didn't care about my list. All I wanted was for my mum and dad to stop fighting.

Chapter 2
The Sad Words

And then I heard the words that made me sadder than a bird without a nest or a puppy without a tail to wag.

"You've killed Christmas."

I didn't understand what Mum meant. 'How can you kill Christmas?' I thought. It isn't alive. How can you kill something that isn't alive?

And then I knew what Mum meant. She meant that Dad had killed FATHER CHRISTMAS.

And I realised something else, even if I couldn't really explain why.

It was my fault.

It was my fault that Dad had killed Father Christmas. And that meant that I had killed Father Christmas.

Chapter 3
Onion in My Eye

I knew that I was crying because my face was all wet. I tried to cry quietly, so nobody would hear me. But I must have made a crying noise.

"Why are you crying, Jo-Jo?"

My baby sister, Poo-face, was standing by the side of my bed. She was hugging her Teddy, and they both looked sad.

"I'm not crying," I said. "I've just got some onion in my eyes."

That's what my mum always says, when she's crying.

"Come on, Poo-face," I said, and I took her by the hand and led her out of the

room. "Let's get you back to bed. The sooner you go to sleep, the sooner Father Christmas will come."

But when I said those words I knew I was going to cry again, so I hurried back to my own bedroom.

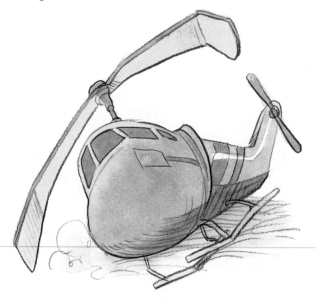

Chapter 4
The Best Idea Ever

Now that I had killed Father Christmas,
I knew that I wouldn't get any of the
toys on my Christmas list. No robot, no
racing car, no helicopter that really flies,
no anything.

But that wasn't what was making me sad. What was making me sad was the hole in the world where Father Christmas used to be.

A fat, happy hole, with a big white beard and a smile in it.

And that's when I had my idea. It was the best idea I'd ever, ever had.

Better than the time I made a parachute from my bed sheet.

Better than the time I decided to live like a monkey for a week and only eat bananas, talk in monkey whoops and wear a monkey tail to school.

If I HAD killed Father Christmas,
then it was my job to fill up the hole in
the world that was left behind. That was
only fair.

I would have to BE Father Christmas.

I didn't have long to think up a plan.
I didn't have any elves to make presents

and wrap them up. I didn't have a sleigh
or a herd of magic reindeer to deliver
them. I was only a little boy.

But every Father Christmas has to
start somewhere. I could start right
here, right now, in my house, in my
street.

Chapter 5
A Pile of Presents

First, the toys ...

I had a whole cupboard full of them,
from Christmases and birthdays long
ago. My bulldozer, my building blocks,
my baby books, my broken bits ...

I piled everything up. It was a lot of
presents. I was going to need two pillow

cases for sacks. I pulled the cases off my
pillows and packed all the presents in.

The pillow cases were heavy and
lumpy.

Perfect!

Chapter 6
A Sort of Superhero

I looked at myself in the mirror. I didn't look even a bit like Father Christmas. I looked like a little boy. That was rubbish.

Father Christmas is a sort of superhero, and every superhero needs a costume.

But I didn't have a costume, except for my old Batman pyjamas, and that would be silly.

I nearly gave up. But then I thought that Father Christmas never gives up. If he gave up, then the whole world would be sad, all the time.

So I did some hard thinking.

The bushy white beard would have to wait till I grew up. And I'd have to eat a lot of dinners if I wanted to be as big and fat as Father Christmas ...

But I had an idea for the rest of my costume.

I sneaked downstairs on my tiptoes, creep, creep, creep.

Mum and Dad had stopped fighting. I could hear the telly in the living room. I went to the coat cupboard, and found my mum's red coat. It looked a little bit like something Father Christmas might wear, if it was dark, and you half closed your eyes. It was so long it trailed on the ground, but that was OK. When I put it on I felt a bit like a king in a play.

I tiptoed back upstairs. I tied a big belt around the outside of the costume – just like Father Christmas.

Now everything was ready.

Chapter 7
My Father Christmas Plan

I was only going to be Father Christmas for our street, but I still had to plan it all out, just like the real Father Christmas. He couldn't deliver one present to Peru and then another to China and another to Brazil. He'd be all over the place, and it would be Boxing Day before some children got their presents.

First I would go to the twins, Penny and Polly, at number 7. They were the sort of girls who don't like dolls. They could have my old football. It was a bit floppy, but you could still kick it.

Next I'd go to number 9, where Samit lives. He's my friend. He could have my bulldozer. The shovel at the front didn't go up and down any more, but apart from that it was a top bulldozer.

And then I'd visit number 14, where James Conway lives. He's my Mortal Enemy, but it's Christmas, so I would give him my best broken bits.

At number 16 there was a baby. I
didn't know its name or if it was a boy
baby or a girl baby. It was just a baby.
So it could have my squidgy book with a
picture of a carrot on every page.

And then I remembered that at number 12 there was an old man called Mr Grouch. That wasn't his real name, but that's what we called him, because he always looked grumpy, as if someone had just stolen his sweets. No wonder he was always alone.

But then I thought that maybe he was grumpy because he didn't have any sweets. I looked in my sweet stash. I had some good sweets and some bad sweets and some sweets that were just OK. I got the bad ones and the OK ones and wrapped them up in a hanky. Then I unwrapped the hanky and put in half of my best sweets, too.

GOOD SWEETS

OK SWEETS

BAD SWEETS

I put the sweets and all the other presents in the pillow case sacks. They looked just right – bulgy and full and happy.

Chapter 8

The Worst Idea Ever

I opened my bedroom window and climbed up onto the window ledge.

Every Christmas I could ever remember had been grey and brown and rainy. But not this one. There was snow everywhere! It must have fallen when

my mum and dad were fighting. Sneaky
snow.

Everything in the world that had
been hard and straight and cruel was
now soft and curvy. And white!

I tried to think of what the snow was
as white as. A swan, a cloud, a glass of
milk? But it was no use. Nothing is as
white as snow.

I looked at the ground below. My plan had been to climb down the drainpipe, but now I knew that the snow would catch me in its soft arms.

It would be like jumping on to a giant marshmallow.

That's what I hoped anyway.

First I threw the big, heavy pillow case
sacks out of the window. They landed
with a WHUMP! in the deep snow.

Now it was my turn. "One-Two-
Three-Jump," I said. I meant to dive out
into the snow the way that a penguin
jumps into the sea.

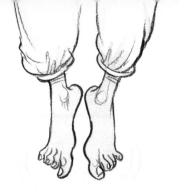

But all of a sudden the ground and the snow seemed a long, long way away, and I was just a teeny-tiny bit scared.

So I decided not to dive out like a penguin after all.

I turned around and climbed out until I was holding on with my fingers, and my legs were dangling in thin air.

It was just then that I decided that being Father Christmas was a Bad Idea. It was cold outside with all that snow, and my fingers were starting to go all tingly and numb.

I decided that I would just climb back inside, put Mum's red coat back in the cupboard and get into bed. Someone else could have Father Christmas's job.

NO!

I had killed Father Christmas. I
would BE Father Christmas.

I let my fingers slide through the
slush on the window ledge.

As I fell backwards into the night I saw something appear at the window.

It was Poo-face.

She stretched her pudgy little arm out towards me.

"NOOOOOOOOOOOO JO-JO," she screamed.

"Bye bye, Poo-face," I said, and I waited to hit the soft snow.

Chapter 9
Ho! Ho! HO!

CRASH!

It wasn't soft. It was hard and
lumpy, and it really hurt!

And it wasn't snow.

I had landed in some kind of cart or bucket or wheelbarrow or ...

"Well, what have we here?"

The voice was deep and gentle and happy, like a big friendly dog.

I looked up into a face full of white hair.

I wanted to scream, but even before the scream came out it had turned into a shout of joy.

"FATHER CHRISTMAS!"

"It is indeed. But don't expect any ho-ho-hos," he said. "I'm already late."

"But I thought I'd, I thought I'd ..."

"Speak up, young man," he boomed.

"I thought I'd killed you," I blurted at last.

"KILLED ME?"

For a second I thought he was angry, but then I realised he was laughing.

"Do I look like I've been killed?"

"Er, no."

"Of course not. You can't kill an idea," he said. "You can't kill a feeling. You can't kill love."

Chapter 10
Hold on Tight

And then I felt the cold wind in my hair, and I knew that we were flying. I had landed right in Father Christmas's sleigh. I looked down and I saw the white world speed by below, and I looked in front of me and I saw 1–2–3–4–5–6–7–8 reindeer straining at their harnesses.

"Is this real?" I asked.

"Can you see the stars?" Father Christmas said.

I looked up.

"Yes."

"Can you feel the wind?"

"Yes."

"Can you smell those dirty old reindeer?"

I sniffed. "Pooooooh! Yes!"

"I told them they needed to have a bath, silly animals!" Father Christmas said. "Anyway, if you can see it and feel it and smell it, then it's real. Now, would you like to fly with me for a little while?"

"Yes please!"

"Hold on tight then!"

Chapter 11
Lights Like Tiny Stars

I clung to the sides of the sleigh, and
Father Christmas cried, "Giddy-up there,
giddy-up now," and we shot ahead, faster
than ever. Faster than a helicopter for
sure. Maybe a little bit slower than a
rocket.

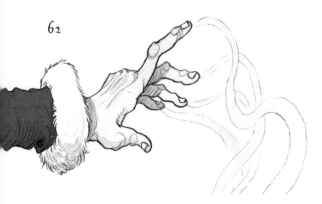

We banked over the houses in my street, and each time we flew over a chimney pot, Father Christmas spread out his hand. It was as if he were giving it a high five. It seemed to me that, as he did this, lights, like tiny stars, poured from his fingers and flowed down the chimneys.

"What are you doing, Father Christmas?" I asked.

"I'm sending love down the chimneys," he said, "so it fills up the houses like water in a hot water bottle."

"But what about the presents …?" I asked.

"The presents?" Father Christmas almost shouted. "LOVE is the present!"

Then I saw for the first time that there weren't any presents inside the sleigh. Not even a single sack.

"But I thought you gave children THINGS ... toys ... helicopters, space rockets, not just love ..."

"Well, I do. The love turns into toys. How else could I fit all those presents in my sleigh?"

So that was it. I'd always wondered how Father Christmas did it.

"You can carry enough love for the whole world in one heart," he said.

Then Father Christmas put his hand over my heart.

"It doesn't matter," he told me, "if it's the heart of a little boy, or the heart of a fat old man."

Chapter 12

Goodbye, Father Christmas

But then I remembered.

"PRESENTS!" I yelled, and I slapped my head. In all the excitement of meeting Father Christmas I'd forgotten about the special presents I'd got ready for everyone. They were still in the sacks in the snow outside my house.

"Can we go and get my presents," I asked, "so we can deliver them together?"

Father Christmas looked down at me and smiled. I could tell from the way his eyes went all crinkly. The mouth part of the smile was hidden inside his big white beard.

"Of course we can," he said, and he pulled on the reins to turn the reindeer back to my house. In a few seconds we were there.

"I'll hover here, over the ground, and you jump down," he said. "Get ready."

Father Christmas helped me climb up on to the edge of the sleigh.

"Steady, steady," he said. "I'll go a bit lower."

I balanced on the edge of the sleigh. It was a bit wobbly.

I looked back at Father Christmas.
He was focused on getting us close to the
ground. I looked down again and saw
my two sacks of presents, lying deep in
the snow.

But looking down was a big mistake. It made me dizzy. The world went topsy-turvy. And down I fell. I looked back one last time, and I saw Father Christmas stretch out his hand, but it was too late. I hit the snow and sank down into it.

I was still falling into the soft whiteness, falling, falling, falling, with the white becoming darker and darker, and then, as I kept falling, it became whiter and whiter again. It felt as though I was falling up and not down into the snow.

And then I heard voices.

"JO-JO! JO-JO!"

It was the voice of Poo-face, who is really called Rosie. And then I heard my dad and my mum, and they weren't fighting any more. I knew that, because it sounded like they were crying.

I opened my eyes, and their faces were gathered around me, all touching each other. But I could see beyond them, and in the sky the love light streamed from the hand of Father Christmas as he waved me goodbye.